Too Slow for Little Cat

by Karen Walberg • illustrated by John Bennett

"I want to ride," says Little Cat.

"I want to go fast!"

"I like this ride," says Mom.

Little Cat says, "Too slow!"

4

"I like this ride," says Dad.

"Too slow!" says Little Cat.

"I want to go fast."

"We like this ride," say Mom and Dad.
"I do NOT like this ride. This ride is
TOO SLOW," says Little Cat.

Little Cat says, "I want to go on THIS ride."

"This ride will be fun," says Little Cat.

"This ride will NOT be fun," say Mom and Dad.

"I like this ride!"
says Little Cat.

"TOO FAST!" say Mom and Dad.